Grandma Gra___ Brave and Tall

written and illustrated by
Antoinette Brooks

Get Exclusive Grandma, Grandma Brave and Tall Material

One of the best things about being a writer is getting to know and share things with my readers.

Why not join my **free** starter library for a **free and exclusive** *Grandma Grandma, Brave and Tall* activity set!

Just visit
www.missbrookslovesbooks.com

ISBN: 978-1-915539-02-1

Bright Thoughts Publishing

Grandma Grandma
Brave and Tall

A story that celebrates the beauty and strength of DIFFERENT grandmothers in one family, from one generation to another... and another...

Dear Reader

When I was a child, my mother used to tell me the most wonderful stories about her childhood in rural Jamaica.

She told me about her dear cousins and friends, but most of all, she shared fascinating stories about her beloved grandmother - and great-grandmother too.

This book is inspired by some of the stories my mother told me.

It begins on a cold London evening.

A small girl is tucked up in bed. Her grandma has whispered goodnight, but she is

VERY DETERMINED

not to go to sleep just yet.

Has that ever happened to you?

So she does exactly what I think you would do. She begs her Grandma for a bedtime story and that is how our tale begins...

"Grandma, Grandma,
brave and tall,
tell me a story of
when you were
small..."

"Hush my child, it's time to sleep.
It's late now and stories can keep.
Close your eyes now you're in bed.
I'll tell you another day instead."

"Grandma, can't you share with me -
just one before-I-go-to-sleep story?"

Grandma is quiet for a while.
Then she gives the warmest smile.
"Aah," she says, "let me see..."

When I was a child, same
size as you,
I grew up in a land where
hummingbirds flew

The smell of hibiscus
was sweet on the breeze
We ate mangoes, pineapples and
sweet neesberries*.

*A sweet, juicy fruit found in the Caribbean

Then my father had a surprise.
"We are moving," he said.
"Five thousand miles."

Five thousand miles
across rough
oceans and seas...

to a strange, new land that
did not know me.

I shivered at night as I lay in bed,
wishing for life back home instead.

I thought of MY grandma by the ackee tree,
and the stories she always shared with me.

The stories she told me whenever I said,
"Grandma, Grandma,
brave and tall,
tell me a story of when
you were small..."

My grandma was quiet awhile. Then she gave the warmest smile. "Aah," she said, "let me see..."

When I was a child, same age as you, I'd go fish with my uncles in their dugout canoe.

But a big war started faraway
and I had to say goodbye to my uncles one day.

The yard was quiet with all of them gone
but my grandma said, "Little One be strong."

I'd curl up close to her, and sitting near,
rest my head on her lap
and as she plaited my hair,
I'd say,

"Grandma, Grandma,
brave and tall,
tell me a story
of when you were small."

My grandma was quiet awhile.
Then she gave the warmest smile.
"Aah," she said, "let me see..."

When I was a girl, same
size as you,
storms raged through
our village.

Violent winds blew!

Mr Hurricane was ANGRY!

Mr Hurricane was MAD!

He flattened our houses.
Tore trees from the
ground.

Pulled me high in the air

and spun me around...

My grandma grabbed
me.
She held me tight.
She hid me in a barrel
for three days and
nights.
She whispered, "Be
brave. The storm will
not last."

When the sun came
back
and the hurricane
passed, I
said, "Grandma,
Grandma,
brave and tall,
tell me a story of
when
you were small."

My grandma was quiet awhile.

Then she gave the warmest smile.

"Aah," she said, "let me see...."

When I was a girl
same size as you,
there was always so much work
we had to do.

Feed goats.
Sweep yard.
Carry wood for the fire.

Milk cows.
Wash clothes.
Hang them up on the wire.

But every August of every year,

we celebrated with our

freedom fair!

Fireworks! Dancing!

Singing all night long. Eating coconut sweets.

Singing Freedom songs

So whether you're lying tucked up in bed
ready to sleep with your dozy head,

Or whether you travel thousands of miles
over oceans and seas and all the world wide,

treasure these tales of where you are from.
Hold them close by as you travel along.

These are stories that
whisper and say, "Yes it's
true.
All these grandmas
were strong.
Their strength is in you."

Now there's one special
thing that I ask you to do.
Share your own stories
with others
as I've shared these with
you.

About the Author

Antoinette Brooks loved creating stories and scribbling pictures from an early age. She studied Economics at the University of London before realising she was a hopeless economist who did not care for maths or figures, and much preferred words and drawings instead.

This book was inspired by the stories her mother told her of growing up with her own grandmother in the Caribbean.

Antoinette says, "I loved hearing the stories of everyday life that my mother and aunt shared with me. Those were wonderful days and times. I treasure all the memories and it is my joy to share some of them with you."

Visit

www.MissBrooksLovesBooks.com

for more exciting stories and goodies!

Other Books by Antoinette Brooks

Motherland, Sweet Motherland

A joyful celebration of the Caribbean childhood of the Windrush generation

For younger readers
The Tippy Tappy Katkins series

Tippy Tappy Katkins: Things I Like to Do

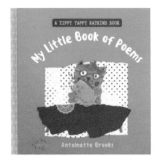

My Little Books of Poems
- Coming Soon!

REVIEWS ARE APPRECIATED!!!

I hope you loved this book. I poured a lot of love into it. If you enjoyed this story, please do leave a review on Amazon.

It means so much to me and helps me share my stories with more readers.

Thank you!

Get Exclusive Grandma, Grandma Brave and Tall Material

One of the best things about being a writer is getting to know and share things with my readers.

Why not join my **free** starter library for a **free and exclusive** Grandma *Grandma, Brave and Tall* activity set!

Just visit
www.missbrookslovesbooks.com

For my mother and father, and also aunt and dear cousins who shared stories of my grandmother and great-grandmother. For my nieces and nephews, I hope you will treasure stories and memories of your own grandma.

Printed in Great Britain
by Amazon

10347098R00020